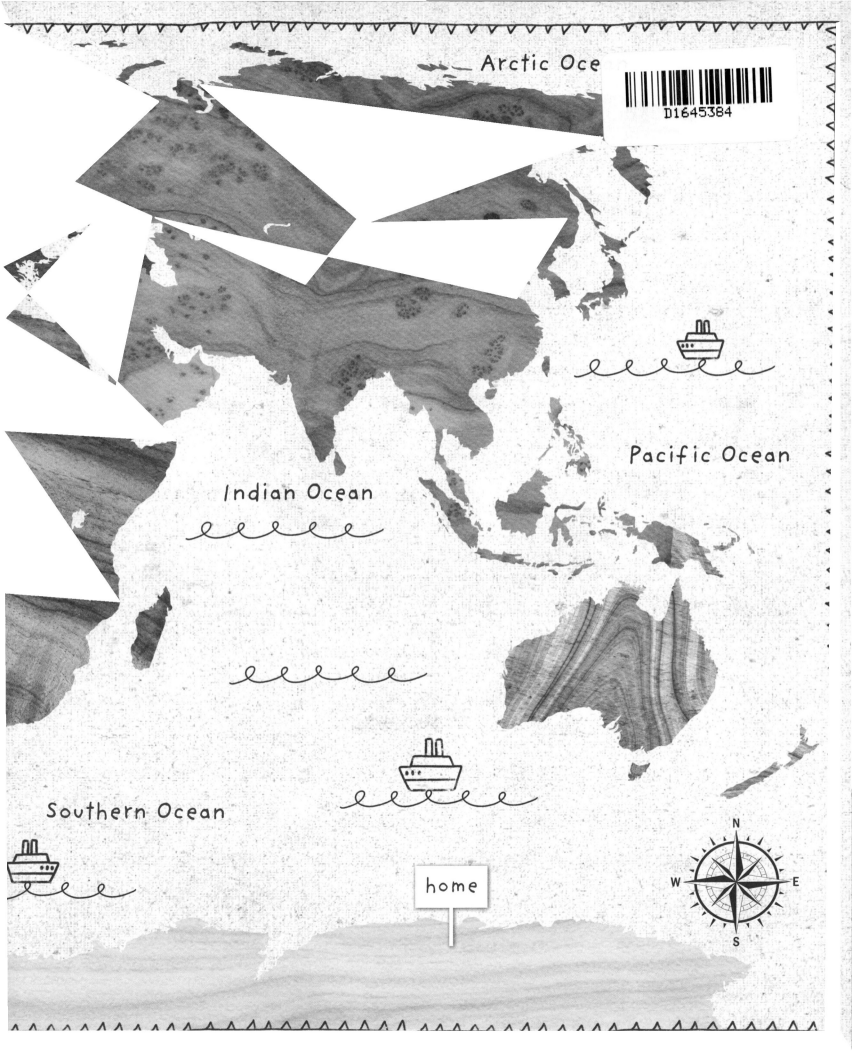

Published in 2021 by Hardie Grant Explore, an imprint of Hardie Grant Publishing

Hardie Grant Explore (Melbourne)
Wurundjeri Country
Building 1, 658 Church Street
Richmond, Victoria 3121

Hardie Grant Explore (Sydney)
Gadigal Country
Level 7, 45 Jones Street
Ultimo, NSW 2007

www.hardiegrant.com/au/explore

 A catalogue record for this book is available from the National Library of Australia

Hardie Grant acknowledges the Traditional Owners of the Country on which we work, the Wurundjeri people of the Kulin Nation and the Gadigal people of the Eora Nation, and recognises their continuing connection to the land, waters and culture. We pay our respects to their Elders past, present and emerging.

Plume: World Explorer
ISBN 9781741177664

10 9 8 7 6 5 4 3 2 1

Publisher
Melissa Kayser
Project editor
Megan Cuthbert
Editor
Irma Gold
Proofreader
Lyric Dodson
Design
Jo Hunt
Typesetting assistance
Megan Ellis

The illustrations in this book were created digitally.

Colour reproduction by Megan Ellis and Splitting Image Colour Studio

Printed in Malaysia

PLUME

world explorer

TANIA MCCARTNEY

Hardie Grant

EXPLORE

This is **Plume**.

Oh wait – he's a bit hard to see.

Let's zoom in.

Hmmm.

Let's zoom in a bit more …

And spin that globe
a little, too …

Okay – that's better.

He's way down here, at the bottom of our planet.
It's the world's largest desert – do you know what it's called?

Antarctica.

It's vast. And frosty. And everything looks the same.

Same sky, same clouds, same ice.

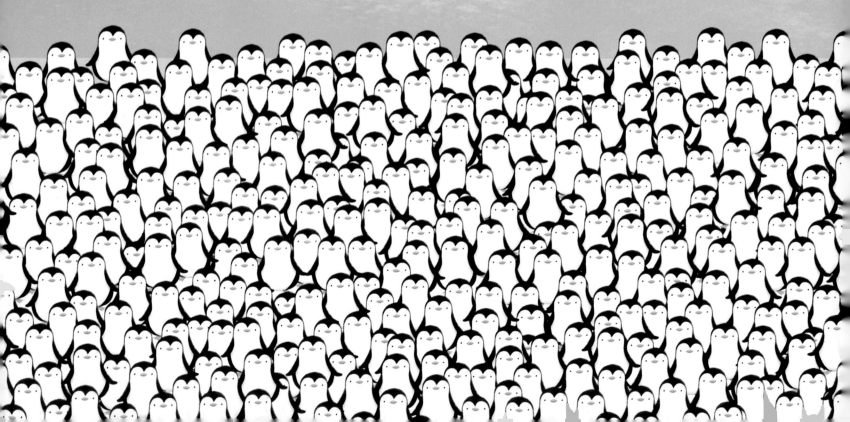

The penguins most **especially** look the same.

Except one.

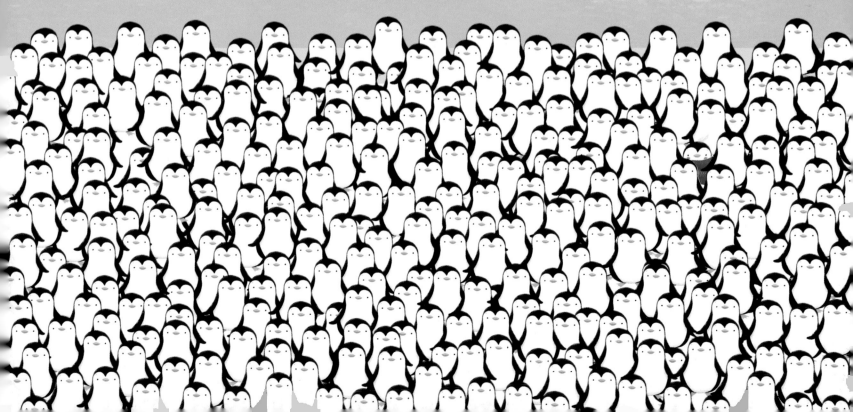

This is **Plume**.

Plume is a little bit **different** to all the other penguins.

He's quite the **dancer**.

He loves a spot of **squash**.

And boy, can this penguin **swim!**

He loves to **skydive**.

He very much loves to **cook**.

And **knit**.

And **colour in**.

He totally rocks a jaunty **ensemble**.

And read. Oh, my, does Plume love to read. And read …

And **read**.

Inside the pages of a book, Plume can travel the world.

He can dive **deep** in search of treasure.

He can climb **high** to touch the sky.

He can feel **big**.

He can feel **small**.

Plume can make friends wherever he goes ...
and discover **a world of rainbows**.

When Plume closes the cover of a book, he returns **home**.

But home can be a very **lonely** place.

So, Plume gets **creative**.

Gelato in every flavour.

Spices for every tongue.

Tunes in every octave.

Yes, Plume is a little bit **different**
to all the other penguins.

Every Wednesday, at a quarter-past-three, the **Albatross Express** arrives in Antarctica.

Plume loves to order **treasure** from around the world. Ava often brings books for Plume, but today she brings...

tea
from **China**

fork-split muffins
from **England**

crayons
from the **USA**

and jandals
from **New Zealand**.

Ava travels far and wide for the Albatross Express.
When she visits Plume, she always stays for
afternoon tea.

Plume puts the kettle on, then settles in for
Ava's tales of faraway places …

where gelato actually **melts**

and **monsters** live in lakes

and birds come in **pink**.

When it's time for Ava to leave,
Plume plonks down on the ice.

He watches her prepare for **take-off**.

How Plume wishes he could take off, too.

Plume is up before the sun.

He puts in a **special order** to the Albatross Express, and this time, he chooses same-day delivery.

He just can't wait.

Ava arrives at a quarter-past-three. She doesn't have long – there's a world of deliveries to make.

Plume takes a tube from her basket. He's ready for take-off, but he wants to leave something **special** behind.

He opens the tube ...

Welcome

... and the **world** spills out.

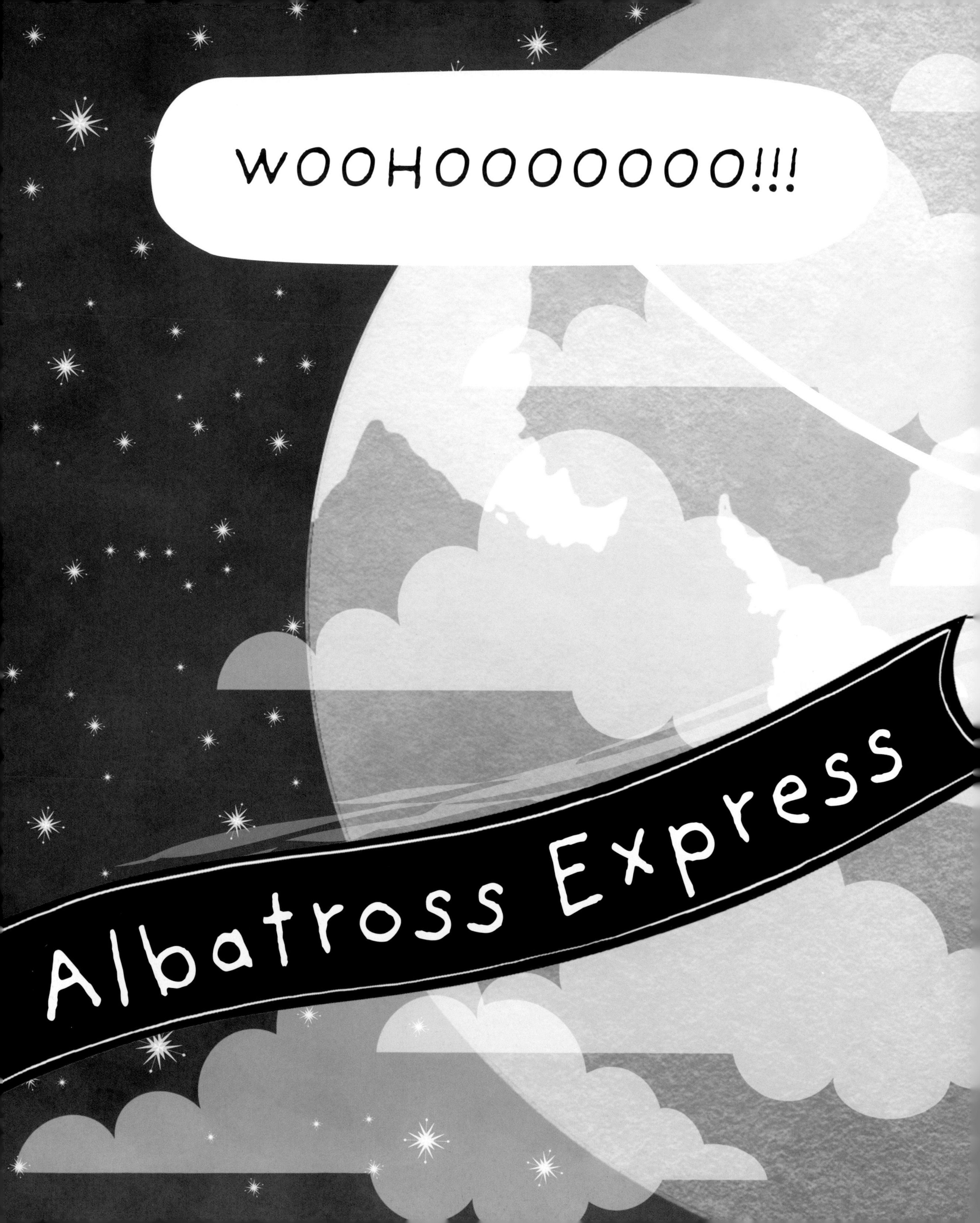
WOOHOOOOOOOO!!!
Albatross Express

Ava lowers the landing gear.
But Plume can't wait.

He dives **deep** in search of treasure.

FIRST STOP!

Next stop is China – home to the world's **greatest wall**.

NI HAO!

Ping takes Plume on an ancient **journey**, with dumplings – called jiaozi – for dinner.

Plume has never felt so **small**.

Ava cruises over France and lands in Paris, the city of light. Plume is so excited, he just might **pop!**

Bienvenue à Paris

BONJOUR!

Lucien treats him to chocolate, melted in a cup.

Plume has never known such **bliss**.

Chocolat CHAUD

In England's capital city, Jasminder meets Plume at the Tower of London. They take the bus with the **best view** in town.

Albatross Express

HIYA!

TURMERIC

LONDON ♔ TOURS

- PICCAD
- OXFORD
- HYDE
- MARBLE

At high tea, Jasminder spices it up. Plume's tongue **tingles** all day long.

In Canada, the great white north, Ojistah welcomes Plume to Kanien'kehá:ka First Nation. She makes him feel right at **home**.

SHÉ:KON!

For morning tea, it's tree sap **drizzled** in the snow.

Plume takes notes.

Next stop is the United States. Plume meets Hamish in New York City, **the Big Apple**. He's astonished to find so many countries in one place.

Plume takes his hot dog with **the works!**

Sol guides Plume over the **mountaintops** of Peru – where sky touches land. Plume closes his eyes and points his beak for home.

¿CÓMO ESTÁS?

TOURS de PERU

They crunch sweet potato chips as they trek, and Sol shows Plume how to **dribble**.

North America
Europe
Africa
Antarctica
ASIA
Oceania

Ava's final delivery takes them over a **rainbow** – to South Africa and the streets of Cape Town.

Siya greets Plume with the gumboot dance. Plume is quite the dancer.

Afterwards, they gobble apricot sweets, baked in the **sun**.

On the way back to Antarctica, Plume's heart feels **bright** – like someone has coloured it in.

Ava lowers the landing gear. But Plume can't wait.

He shares his tales of faraway places.

How he travelled **deep** in search of treasure
and climbed **high** to touch the sky.

How he felt so very **big** and completely **small**.

And very best of all … how he found **a world of rainbows**.

Things have always been so **black and white**.
The penguins have never seen a rainbow like this before.

Plume brings out the crayons...
and shows the penguins how
to **colour in**.

He's hoping they can learn to make **rainbows**.

It may take some **time** …

Ava packs up her basket. She has a full day of deliveries to prepare. But right before take-off, she **stops**.

She looks at Plume.

She **smiles**.

for Connor

TANIA MCCARTNEY

is an author, illustrator, editor and designer, with a library the size of Antarctica. The creator of picture books, junior fiction, non-fiction, maps, puzzles and two travel-loving kids, she is also the founder of the acclaimed Kids' Book Review, and The Happy Book Podcast. With a deep love of maps and travel (and coffee!), she has lived in France, England and China … and now lives in a Land Down Under with a forest of artwork, a mountain of books and a rather itchy travel bug.
www.taniamccartney.com

THANK YOU

Like all books, *Plume* would not be possible without a village of magical book makers, squirreling away behind the scenes. Enormous thanks to my visionary publisher Melissa Kayser and our core team – Jo Hunt, Irma Gold and Megan Cuthbert. Huge thanks to Alyson O'Brien and Astrid Browne, as well as our brilliant local advisors for their invaluable input. And lastly, to my amazing husband and kids for their endless support, patience … and love of travel.